DOMINOES

Mystery in Muscat

LEVEL ONE   400 HEADWORDS

OXFORD
UNIVERSITY PRESS

ISBN: 978 0 19 424916 4   Book
ISBN: 978 0 19 424914 0   Book and MultiROM Pack
MultiROM not available separately

Printed in China

This book is printed on paper from certified and well-managed sources

ACKNOWLEDGEMENTS

Cover image: Corbis/Walter Bibikow

Illustrations by: Sebastian Camagajevac

*The publisher would like to thank the following for their kind permission to reproduce photographs and
other copyright material*: Alamy pp.0 (Beirut/F1online digitale Bildagentur GmbH), 0 (Muscat/
Justin Kase zninez), 7 (pink crayons/imagebroker), 7 (clothes/MARKA), 7 (sea turtle/Photoshot
Holdings Ltd), 19 (Muscat/Jon Arnold Images Ltd), 30 (painting/eMotionQuest), 30 (steal/Mark
Bourdillon), 30 (balcony/Hemis), 30 (lock/Kevin Britland), 30 (mountain/BANANA PANCAKE),
38 (mountains in Oman/INTERFOTO), 42 (Wadi Ghul/Eric Nathan), 42 (Nizwa mosque/Image
Source), 42 (Wadi Shab oasis/Tom Till), 42 (Palace and fort/Tibor Bognar), 42 (Mirbat/Dieter
Wertz), 42 (Sharqiya sands/Christine Osborne Pictures), 44 (Edinburgh Castle./Justin Kase
zsixz); The Bridgeman Art Library pp.40 (*Lady with a Red Hat*/Art Gallery and Museum,
Kelvingrove, Glasgow, Scotland/© Culture and Sport Glasgow (Museums), p.41 (Mary Amelia/
Private Collection/The Bridgeman Art Library); Getty pp.30 (A satellite navigator/Nick Koudis),
39 (Arabian Sea turtle/Zena Holloway); Corbis pp.39 (Rolls Royce/ANDY RAIN/epa); Oxford
University Press pp.0 (London/Sydney), 7 (dolphin), 7 (twins).

DOMINOES

Series Editors: Bill Bowler and Sue Parminter

Mystery in Muscat

Julie Till

Illustrated by Sebastian Camagajevac

Julie Till was born and grew up in Liverpool in the north of England. She has lived and worked in the Middle East for over twenty years as a journalist, a teacher, an author, and a teacher-trainer. She has run workshops for teachers in many countries, including Yemen, Syria, Egypt, and Morocco. Her husband is Lebanese and they have one son. She now lives in Dubai, but often travels for work. She enjoys speaking Arabic as she travels around the countries of the Middle East. In her free time she likes to read. She has also written *The Drive to Dubai* for Dominoes.

OXFORD
UNIVERSITY PRESS

BEFORE READING

1 **The people in this story live in Oman, but come from different countries. Match each photo with two phrases.**

1 London, England

2 Beirut, Lebanon

3 Sydney, Australia

4 Muscat, Oman

a [4] It's next to the Arabian Sea.

b [ ] It's not very hot in summer.

c [ ] It's near the Tasman Sea.

d [ ] It's very hot from June to October.

e [ ] It's next to the Mediterranean Sea.

f [ ] It's on the River Thames.

g [ ] Many people there speak Arabic, English, and French.

h [ ] It's hot from November to February.

2 **What mysteries do you read about in this story? Tick three boxes.**

> **mystery** /ˈmɪstri/ *noun* (*pl.* **-ies**)
> Something that is difficult or impossible to understand or explain.

a [ ] Why do two men want to kill an English woman on holiday in Muscat?

b [ ] Why do the airport security guards want to find a woman in red?

c [ ] Why do two boys go to a party in a big hotel to talk to an English minister?

d [ ] Why do some thieves put a painting in a house in the mountains?

e [ ] Why does a black car drive after an English family in the mountains?

f [ ] Where do some thieves put the Sultan's expensive silver dagger?

Chapter 1 ❖ A new country

I didn't want to come to Oman. I was happy back home in England with my friends. I didn't have any friends in Oman. My mum didn't listen. 'It's going to be **boring** in Oman,' I said. 'No friends, and nothing to do.' My sister Sarah was angry, too. She didn't want to leave *her* friends. But it was no good. My dad had work in Muscat, the **capital** of Oman. So we went.

We arrived in Muscat at ten o'clock at night – and it was hot. Most men wore white: a long, white dress – it was called a 'thobe', my mum said – and a little white hat. Everything was very different from England.

A man helped us with our bags. A car was there for us with a driver. We got in, and he drove off.

boring not interesting

capital the most important city in a country

It was dark, and I was tired. I closed my eyes. I didn't want to see Oman. I wasn't interested. After about thirty or forty minutes, the car stopped suddenly. We were at our new house. It was big and white, with a garden at the front and back. We carried our bags into the house. My dad brought two cold drinks for Sarah and me. Mum went upstairs to make our beds ready. When I went upstairs, the **air conditioning** was on in my room. It was wonderful to feel cold again! I changed my **clothes**, got into bed, and soon slept.

I opened my eyes early the next morning. Why was everything white? Where was I? Why was there nothing in my room? Then I remembered. I closed my eyes, but I couldn't sleep again. I got up. When I went downstairs, I saw my mum and sister at the breakfast table.

I ate my breakfast with them. The bread was different here. 'Everything's different,' I thought.

'I have lots of things to do today,' said my mum. 'You can help me or you can go to the **swimming pool** across the road. But it's best to go now before it's very hot.'

Sarah and I ran upstairs and found our things. We didn't want to stay in our new house! Five minutes later, Mum, Sarah, and I went across the road. There were about forty buildings there – **flats**, not houses. They were white and not very tall. There was one flat on the **ground floor** and a second flat on the **first floor** in every building. And every building had a little garden in front and a bigger garden at the back, too.

'You can come here often,' said Mum. 'This swimming pool is for the people in these flats and our house, too. The sea's over there, but it's better to come here when it's hot.'

There were some more children at the swimming pool. First I saw a boy and a girl. The two of them were about twelve or thirteen. They had dark hair and dark eyes. Then I saw a girl with them. She was a year or two younger than them. She had red hair, and a **pink** face.

My mum looked at the children, and then looked at us.

'You see, Jamie, you can make new friends here in Muscat,' she said noisily. 'They're nice children. You can go and play with them.'

I looked down at my feet. My face was very pink. The children in the swimming pool looked at us. The older girl smiled. Perhaps she felt sorry for us. My mum gave Sarah and me two bottles of cold water and left. It was only ten o'clock, but it was very hot.

We quickly went into the swimming pool. The water was wonderfully cold. I **swam** up and down. I wanted to make

swim (*past* **swam**) to go through the water moving your arms and legs

4

new friends, but it wasn't easy. I don't like talking to people for the first time. But then the girl with the pink face swam over to Sarah and me.

'Hi, I'm Ruth. I'm from Australia. I moved here six months ago. My mum and dad work at one of the big hotels here. Those two are my friends. They're from Lebanon. He's called Taymour and she's called Nadine. We come to the swimming pool every day in the summer. They arrived here about two years ago. They speak Arabic, English, and French. I'm learning Arabic, but I can't say a lot. That's good for my Arabic teacher, my mum says. Usually I talk a lot! What are your names?' she asked, and then she stopped speaking. So we told her.

Taymour and Nadine swam nearer. They were **twins**, and they were thirteen.

'Do you like it here in Oman?' I asked.

'Yes, it's nice. I like the winter. It's very hot now, but in the winter it's good. Sometimes we stay all weekend by the sea. There's a lot to do in the winter,' said Taymour.

'You can see **turtles** and swim with **dolphins**,' said Ruth.

'The weather is better here in a month or two. It's colder then,' said Taymour.

'What do you do now, in the summer?' I asked.

'There isn't much to do. We come to the swimming pool every day. A lot of people leave Oman in the summer because it's very hot here. We were in Lebanon earlier this month and we came back only last week. It's very quiet here in the summer. Nothing much happens when it's very hot,' said Taymour.

But he was wrong. Very wrong!

READING CHECK

1 Complete the sentences with the names of the people in Chapter 1.

Jamie   Nadine   Ruth   Sarah   Taymour

a It's ....*Jamie*.... and ....'s first day in Oman. They are from England.

b .... and .... are twins. They are from Lebanon.

c .... is from Australia.

2 Are these sentences true or false? Tick the boxes.

	True	False
a Jamie and Sarah are in Oman because their father is working there.	✔	☐
b They feel excited about living in a different country.	☐	☐
c They go to a swimming pool across the road from their house.	☐	☐
d In the pool, a boy with red hair speaks to them.	☐	☐
e Ruth's family moved to Oman a year ago.	☐	☐
f Taymour likes living in Oman.	☐	☐
g There isn't much to do in Oman in summer because it's hot.	☐	☐

WORD WORK

1 Use words from Chapter 1 to label the picture.

2 Match the words with the pictures.

clothes   pink   twins   turtle   ~~dolphin~~

a ...*dolphin*...

b ....

c ....

d ....

e ....

GUESS WHAT

What happens in the next chapter? Tick two boxes.

a ☐ Jamie goes to Taymour's house to play in the afternoon.

b ☐ The two boys go into the garden of one of the flats.

c ☐ They see two men kill a woman in a first floor flat.

d ☐ The two men make a lot of money.

e ☐ The boys go to the police and tell their story.

Chapter 2 ✧ The garden

At twelve my mum arrived at the swimming pool.

'Can you come to my house this afternoon?' asked Taymour quietly. 'Ask your mum. We can play on my computer there.'

After we ate, I asked her.

'Well, I'm going to the shops this afternoon with Sarah,' my mum said. 'So, yes, you can go to Taymour's house. But be home by four o'clock, Jamie. Don't be late!'

So I went to Taymour's house, and we played on his computer. Then his mum called him.

'Don't forget, Taymour. You must **water** Tom's garden today. You didn't do it yesterday. Go and do it now.'

'Come on, Jamie,' said Taymour. 'You can help. Tom is our **neighbour**. He comes from Scotland, and he goes back there every summer. We must water the flowers in his garden every day when he isn't here. Well, *I* must! My mum never asks Nadine. It's always me.'

'I understand, Taymour. My sister never does any work. It's always me, too!'

We went to Tom's garden. Tom lived on the ground floor in the last building. There were two ground floor flats between Taymour's flat and Tom's flat. There were no flats on the right of Tom's flat.

'Nobody lives in the flats next to Tom,' Taymour told me. 'They left Oman and went back home. But there's somebody new in the flat over Tom's flat. I don't know him. But he's English, my mum says.'

There was a **hose** in Tom's garden. Taymour took it in his hand. 'Oh, I don't like watering the garden,' Taymour said, and he looked at me, 'but I love watering people!'

water to put water on, or give water to something

neighbour a person who lives near you

hose a long thing that brings water from the house to the garden

'Aaargh! Get off,' I cried, and I ran up and down the garden. Taymour ran after me. The water from the hose was cold. My clothes were soon **wet**. My hair was wet. My legs and feet were wet. Everything was wet.

I ran to the water **tap**, took off the hose and put a **bucket** under the tap. When there was lots of water in the bucket, I took it in my hand and ran after Taymour. Whoosh! Now he was wet, too. I ran with the bucket back to the tap. We ran up and down the garden for a time. The two of us were wet now, and we couldn't stop laughing.

'Stop. I'm tired,' I said in the end. 'I need to sit down.'

There were two old garden chairs near the door to Tom's flat, out of the hot sun. Taymour and I went and sat down on them. I closed my eyes for five minutes. I opened them when I heard two men in the first floor flat over our heads.

wet with water on it

tap water comes out of this in a house

bucket you can carry water in this

'Nobody can hear us, George. The man in the flat under us is in Scotland. Nobody is living in the flats next door. Nothing happens here in the summer. We came here for that,' said one of the men.

I looked at Taymour, but said nothing. I wanted to hear the two men. We needed to stay quiet. Taymour understood.

'When is she arriving, Martin?' asked the second man.

'This weekend. From London to Muscat.'

'How long is she in Oman for?' asked the second man.

'Ten days. And then they want to take her back home.'

'Ah, yes,' the man said with a laugh. 'But she's not going back to London. They're never going to see her again – here or back home in England!'

'When we finish here, I'm taking the money and I'm going to have a nice, long, expensive holiday.'

'I'm going to buy a house by the sea – a big, expensive house!'

'Of course! But let's go in now. It's very hot out here. I need a cold drink.'

The door upstairs opened and then closed. I looked at Taymour. We got up and we walked out of the garden very quietly. We didn't speak. We walked quickly back to Taymour's flat, opened the door and went to his room. He closed the door behind us.

'Did you hear that? They're going to kill someone!' said Taymour. 'Perhaps someone famous.'

'I know. It's **terrible**. They're going to kill a woman when she arrives here in Muscat. Her family isn't going to see her again,' I said.

'Somebody's going to give them a lot of money for this. So they're **hit men**!'

'What can we do? Shall we go to the **police** and tell them about the two men?' Taymour asked.

'I don't know. Are they going to listen to us? Are they going to **believe** our story?'

'You're right. **Adults** never listen,' said Taymour. 'The police are going to tell us: "You're only **kids** and this is a kid's story!"'

'And who are these men going to kill? We don't know. Let's learn more first. Who is she? Why do they want to kill her? Then we can go to the police,' I said.

'Let's tell Nadine. She can help us,' said Taymour. 'And Ruth. Her mum and dad meet lots of important people. Perhaps they know this woman.'

'OK,' I said, and I looked at my watch. 'But I must go home now. Let's all meet tomorrow morning. We don't have much time to help this woman!'

READING CHECK

Complete the sentences with the correct words and names.

first floor flat	garden	~~Jamie~~	London	Muscat
Ruth	Taymour	tired	water	woman

a That afternoon ..... *Jamie* .... goes to play at Taymour's house.

b Taymour goes and works in a neighbour's ....

c The boys play with some .... in the garden.

d They sit down in the garden because they are ....

e They hear two men in the ....

f The men talk about the visit of a woman from London to ....

g 'She isn't going to go back to ....,' they say.

h The boys go back to ....'s house.

i Two men want to kill a .... in Muscat, they think.

j They want to ask Nadine and .... to help.

WORD WORK

1 Find five more words from Chapter 2 in the wordsquare.

c	t	a	p	i	j	a
h	j	m	o	n	e	d
o	p	u	l	d	p	u
s	o	f	i	n	k	l
e	b	u	c	k	e	t
r	r	l	e	b	o	h
k	i	d	r	u	k	e

2 Use the words from Activity 1 to label the pictures.

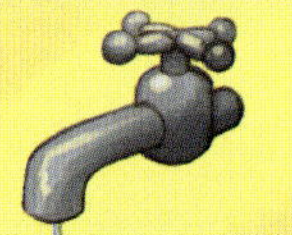

a ..... *hose* .....

b ....

c ....

d ....

e ....

f ....

3 Circle the correct words to complete the sentences about the story.

a Taymour waters / watches the flowers in Tom's garden.

b Tom is a neighbour / next door of Taymour's family.

c Taymour and Jamie are soon very wet / well in the garden.

d 'It's terribly / terrible that they're going to kill a woman,' says Jamie.

e The police never begin / believe children's stories, thinks Jamie.

f The boys want to tell the girls about the hit-men / he-men in the flat.

GUESS WHAT

What happens in the next chapter? Tick one box.

a ☐ The children talk to the police about the hit-men.

b ☐ The boys find the woman from London in the neighbour's flat.

c ☐ One of the hit-men makes friends with Nadine and Taymour's mother.

Chapter 3 — The mystery woman

'Hit-men here in Muscat!' said Ruth the next morning when we told her. 'I can't believe it! This woman's **in danger**. We must **save** her. But how can we? It's a **mystery**.'

'Yes, it is a mystery, but let's think for a minute. What do we know?' I said. 'A woman is coming to Muscat from England this weekend. She's famous, we think. She's staying here for ten days and then going back to England. But in those ten days those men are going to kill her.'

'Well, which famous women are coming to Muscat this weekend? We need to **find out** ...,' said Nadine.

'Let's go to our house,' she said. 'You two can look on the computer. Perhaps you can find out something on the **Internet**. Sarah, Ruth, and I can look in the **newspaper**. Perhaps there's something about her in the *Oman Times*.'

But after half an hour, we stopped looking. There was nothing on the Internet or in the newspaper.

'It's all about today and yesterday, not about things this weekend,' said Nadine.

Ruth looked at her watch. 'I must go home for lunch,' she said, 'but I'm going to ask my **parents**. Perhaps they know. Meet you back at the swimming pool later. About five o'clock.'

In the afternoon, we stayed at home. We didn't go out because it was very hot. At five o'clock we walked across the road to the swimming pool. When we came near it, we could see Ruth, Nadine, and Taymour. They were there before us. They smiled. They knew something!

'I asked my mum and dad,' said Ruth. 'The **Minister for Culture and the Arts** is arriving from England on Friday, they said...'

'And she's a woman!' said Nadine excitedly.

'There's a big **art exhibition** here. She's coming for that,' said Ruth.

'So we found the mystery woman. Good work!' I said.

'But it's not going to be easy to save her,' said Taymour.

We stopped smiling. Taymour was right. How *could* we stop the hit-men?

'Let's tell our parents everything,' said Nadine. 'Then they can tell the police.'

'They're not going to believe us,' I said.

'Jamie's right,' said Sarah.

'But we must do something. So I say let's talk to my mum,' said Taymour.

'She's going to be home in about ten minutes. We can tell her when she arrives,' said Nadine.

We sat in their garden, out of the sun, and we waited for their mum. In the end, we heard her car and then we saw her.

'Mum, we've got something important to tell you,' said Nadine and Taymour, at the same time. And then they stopped.

There was a man behind their mother. He had three big bags in his hands.

'Oh? What's that? Kids, this is Mr Williams. He lives in the flat over Tom's flat. He saw me with these bags by my car. I went to the shops earlier, so there was a lot to carry. He helped me – carried all my bags from the car. Now don't stand there. Taymour, Nadine, take the bags off him!'

She smiled at Mr Williams. 'Thank you for your help,' she said. 'It was very nice of you.'

'I'm happy to help a neighbour,' he smiled. 'Bye, kids!' he said when he left.

'It's good to have nice neighbours. Mr Williams helped your mum with her car this morning, too, Ruth. He always says "hello" and "good morning". What a nice man! Now what did you want to tell me?'

'Erm, nothing important,' said Taymour, quickly.

'Well, take those bags in for me. Are you hungry? Would you like something to eat?' she asked.

When their mum was in the flat, we began **whispering**.

'He's one of the hit-men,' said Taymour.

'So Mr Hit-man is now Mr Nice Neighbour!' I said.

'Which one was he?' asked Sarah.

'He wanted to go in for a cold drink,' I said.

'Well, we can't tell our mum now. "Your nice neighbour is a hit-man!" She isn't going to believe that,' said Taymour.

'No. You're right about that,' said Nadine. 'I know! Let's go and speak to the minister. We can tell her about the killers.'

'But the exhibition opens on Sunday. Why is she coming on Friday?' I asked.

'My dad told me,' said Ruth. 'There's a **party** for the **Sultan** and the VIPs – you know – Very Important People – on Saturday. They can meet and talk, and see the pictures then. Of course, the minister is going to be at that party.'

'So let's tell her when she arrives,' said Sarah.

'Hmm. We can't speak to her at the airport. Think of the police and all the airport **security guards**. We're never going to walk past all of them,' said Taymour.

'What about this party?' I asked. 'Can we talk to her there? Where's it going to be?'

'The art exhibition is at one of the big hotels,' said Ruth. 'It's of Omani and British pictures. My mum and dad are going to the party.'

'Are you going?' I asked.

'No. It's for adults only.'

'Right. But we can talk to her before she goes into the party,' I said. 'Before the hit-men kill her!'

security guard
someone who watches a building and stops bad people from going in

READING CHECK

Correct the mistakes in these sentences.

a A famous woman is staying in Muscat for ten days, the ~~police~~ *children* think.

b They look on the Internet and in newspapers for something about a famous picture.

c Ruth's mother and father tell her about a famous woman from America.

d They want to tell Taymour and Nadine's father about the hit-men.

e One of the kids is helping Nadine's mother with her bags.

f The new neighbour is a terrible man, Nadine's mother thinks.

g The children want to talk to the famous woman at the airport.

h The woman is visiting Oman because she wants to see some people in an art exhibition.

WORD WORK

1 Circle nine more words from Chapter 3 in the picture.

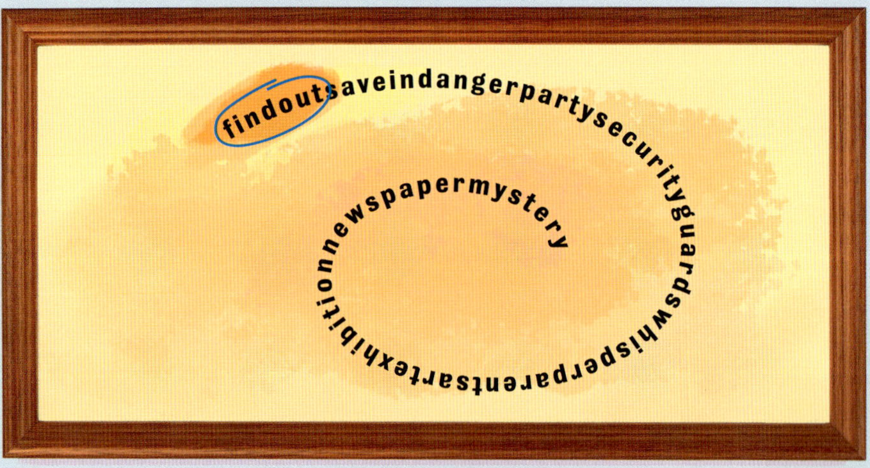

2 Use the words from Activity 1 to complete the sentences.

a We need to ..... *find* .... *out* ...... the woman's name.

b I'm having a birthday .... on Saturday. Can you come?

c I read the story in today's ....

d At the airport, the .... look at your things.

e We must .... the woman.

f I saw a beautiful picture at the .... yesterday.

g The woman is .... , the children think.

h No one knows what happened to the *Mary Celeste*. It's a ....

i Ruth asks her .... about the famous woman.

j Please .... Nobody must hear us!

GUESS WHAT

What happens in the next chapter? Tick the boxes.

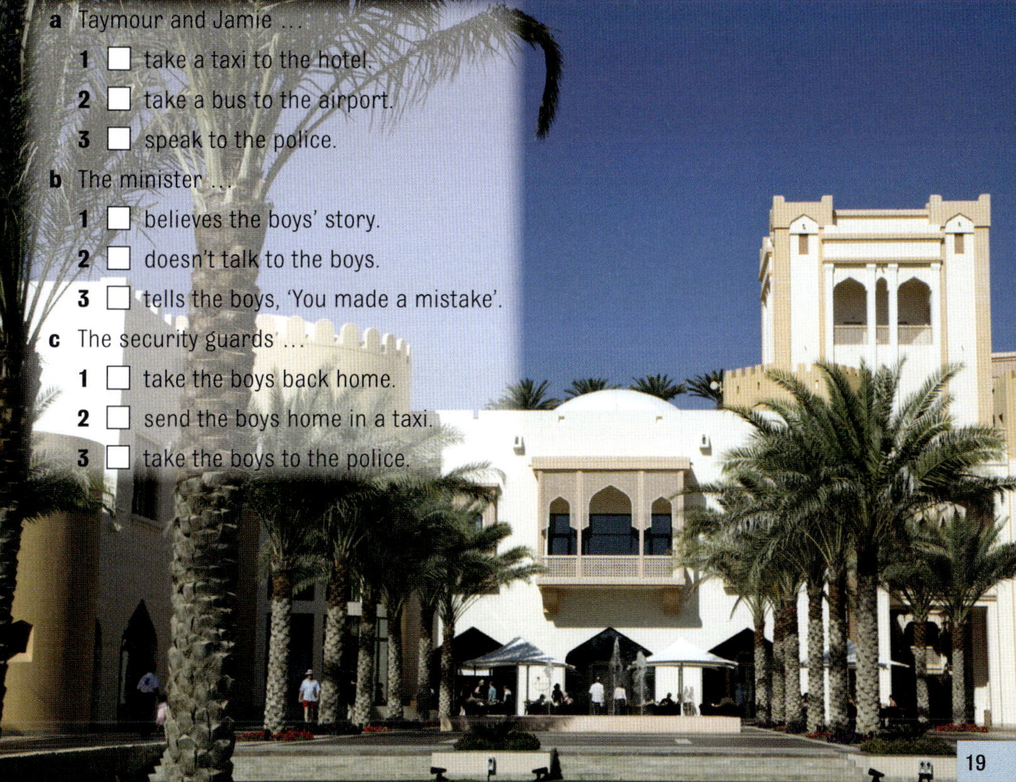

a Taymour and Jamie …
  1 ☐ take a taxi to the hotel.
  2 ☐ take a bus to the airport.
  3 ☐ speak to the police.

b The minister …
  1 ☐ believes the boys' story.
  2 ☐ doesn't talk to the boys.
  3 ☐ tells the boys, 'You made a mistake'.

c The security guards …
  1 ☐ take the boys back home.
  2 ☐ send the boys home in a taxi.
  3 ☐ take the boys to the police.

Chapter 4 — The hotel

'Mum, I'm going over to Taymour's house. Back about nine o'clock,' I said.

'Don't be late,' said my mum.

'Mum, I'm going over to Jamie's house. Back about nine o'clock,' said Taymour in his house.

'Don't be late,' said his mum.

It wasn't right, we knew. 'But we must stop those men and save the minister,' I said. 'Our parents are going to understand in the end – when the police find the killers!'

We took a taxi to the hotel. The party began at 7.30 p.m., but we arrived at the hotel at 6.30 p.m. We wanted to be early. There were a lot of **police officers** on the road in front of the hotel. They stopped our taxi, and looked in the back of the car and under it.

police officer
a man or woman that works for the police

There were more security guards at the door of the hotel. One of them said something in Arabic to Taymour and he answered. The man **nodded** his head and we walked in.

'What did you say to him?' I asked Taymour.

'I said, "Dad's down by the sea with the car. We're staying at the hotel."'

There were lots of nice big chairs in the hotel. We sat near the door. We could see people when they came in and went out. After some time, lots of people began to arrive for the party. We looked carefully at everybody. They were in their best clothes. Most men wore white thobes with beautiful **silver daggers**. 'They wear them only on very important days,' said Taymour. The minister's picture was on the Internet, so we knew her face. We looked at our watches. It was now 7.25 p.m.

'Where is she? Perhaps she's not coming,' I said.

'Perhaps she's dead,' he whispered.

I didn't say a thing. There wasn't time. Just then, there was a lot of noise and a lot of people at the door of the hotel. Some big, tall men came in first — security guards. Then some Omani VIPs. And then she arrived – the Minister for Culture and the Arts. It was time to speak to her. I was afraid, but there was no time to think. Taymour and I walked quickly across to her.

'Minister, minister,' I called.

'Mrs Summers,' cried Taymour.

The security guards began walking over to us.

'Mrs Summers, we must speak to you. Only two minutes please,' I called.

The security guards were in front of us now.

'Mrs Summers! It's very important,' cried Taymour.

nod to move your head up and down

silver an expensive white metal

dagger a knife for killing people (in the old days)

The security guards put their hands on our arms.

'Minister,' I cried, 'we need to talk to you now.'

One security guard **checked** my arms, legs, and back. The second guard checked Taymour.

'Nothing, Mrs Summers. They're OK,' they said.

The minister walked over to us. I was afraid, but we had our two minutes with her.

'Mrs Summers, my friend and I were in a garden. We **overheard** a **conversation** between two men. They're going to kill you.'

'Going to kill me? They said that?' she asked.

'Well, no. But they said: "A famous woman is coming from England at the end of the week – to stay in Oman for ten days. But she's not going to go back to England. Nobody is going to see her again!"'

check to look carefully at something to see that everything is ok

overhear (*past* **overheard**) to hear people talking without them knowing that you are there

conversation when two or more people are talking

The minister nodded. She looked at one of the security guards – the most important one, I think. Then she looked back at us again.

'Did they say my name?' she asked.

'No,' Taymour and I said at the same time.

'Did they say any name?' she asked.

'No,' we said.

'How are they going to kill me? Did they say?'

'No,' I answered.

'They didn't say "kill" but they said: "She's not going back to England,"' said Taymour.

'That's true,' said the minister. 'After Oman, I'm going to China. But I'm not here for ten days. I leave tomorrow morning. So, you see, your story isn't right. You made a mistake, boys.'

'Kids!' said the security guard, and he laughed.

'Thank you. You wanted to help, but be careful,' smiled the minister. 'It isn't easy when you overhear a conversation. You can easily make a **mistake**. Now it's time for me to go. Good night, boys.' And she walked away.

'But, but ...,' I said. But she didn't want to listen any more. Two security guards had our arms and we couldn't move. They asked us, 'Where do you live?' and then they took us to the hotel door. They called a taxi for us. Before we got in it, they told us, 'Never come back to this hotel again!'

'My parents are going to kill me,' said Taymour.

'We can't tell them. I don't want to stay home for a month because my parents are angry with me,' I said.

'But, Jamie, why were we wrong? How did we make a mistake?' asked Taymour.

I didn't have an answer.

mistake when you do something wrong, but you don't know it

READING CHECK

Match the two parts of these sentences.

a	Jamie tells his mum,	**1**	in some big chairs near the door.
b	Taymour tells his mum,	**2**	a security guard at the hotel door.
c	The two boys	**3**	about the conversation between the two men.
d	Taymour speaks Arabic to	**4**	'I'm going to Taymour's house.'
e	The boys wait for the minister	**5**	their mistake.
f	When the minister walks in	**6**	take a taxi to the big hotel.
g	The boys tell the minister	**7**	'I'm going to Jamie's house.'
h	The minister tells the boys,	**8**	call a taxi for the boys.
i	The security guards	**9**	the boys call her name.
j	The boys can't understand	**10**	'You made a mistake.'

WORD WORK

1 Unscramble the letters to make words from Chapter 4.

a o.fficers......

b c.................

c c.................

d d.................

e m.................

f n.................

g o.................

h s.................

2 Complete Jamie's diary with the words from Activity 1 in the correct form.

What a terrible evening! When we got to the hotel, there were lots of police a) ...officers... there. They b) .... under our taxi. Taymour and I waited a long time and then people began to arrive for the party. Many of the men had c) ....

At half past seven, the minister arrived and we called her name. She walked over to us and d) .... at the security guard. Quickly we told her about the two men and their e) .... 'We were in the garden and we f) .... them,' I said. She listened, but she didn't believe us. She's leaving Oman tomorrow. How did we make this terrible g) .... ?

GUESS WHAT

What happens in the next chapter? Tick two boxes.

a The hit-men kill the minister. ☐

b Some people take a picture from the art exhibition. ☐

c The children tell the police about Mr Williams. ☐

d The children go to Mr Williams's flat and look for the picture. ☐

e Mr Williams comes home when Jamie is in his flat. ☐

f The children give the picture to Mrs Summers. ☐

Chapter 5   Mr Williams's flat

Sarah was in her room. She wanted to hear everything. So I told her all about our conversation with the minister.

'Did you **imagine** that conversation between the two men in the garden?' she asked.

'No! Taymour heard them too. I'm going to my room!'

The next morning I didn't go to the swimming pool. I wasn't happy. I didn't want to see Taymour, Nadine, or Ruth. I asked the same questions again and again, 'Why were we wrong? What are those two men going to do? Who are they going to kill?' Yesterday's newspaper was on the breakfast table. There was a story about the art exhibition. I began to read: *'The exhibition is on for ten days. Then the pictures go back to London. The most expensive picture is a **painting** of a woman in a black dress.'* I looked at the little black and white picture. I thought about the conversation between the two men.

'When is she arriving?'

'This weekend. From London to Muscat.'

'How long is she in Oman for?'

'Ten days. And then they want to take her back home.'

'Ah, yes. But she's not going back to London. They're never going to see her again – here or back home in England!'

Of course! Not a woman – but a *painting* of a woman!

I put on my shoes and ran to the swimming pool. Sarah, Nadine, and Taymour were there.

'First, hit-men. Now, **thieves**. Are you right about this? We don't want to make a second mistake,' said Sarah.

Suddenly we heard Ruth.

'Jamie, Sarah, Nadine, Taymour!' she cried. She ran over to us. Her face was pink and hot.

imagine to see or hear something in your head that is not true

painting a coloured picture

thief (*plural* **thieves**) a person who takes things without asking

'It's a painting!' she cried.

'We know, but how do you know?' asked Nadine.

'My mum phoned my dad. She went to the art exhibition this morning. Thieves took a painting late last night. It's the most expensive picture.'

'Do you think it's in Mr Williams's flat?' asked Nadine.

'Let's see. I saw Mr Williams about an hour ago,' said Taymour. 'He got into his car and drove away. Let's go back to Tom's garden.'

It was very quiet in the garden. The flat over it was quiet, too. We stood and looked up at it.

'Let's **climb** up,' said Nadine. 'Bring the table over here. We can put a chair on it and climb over the **balcony**.'

'I can climb up,' said Taymour.

'No, I'm the tallest. I can do it,' I said.

A few minutes later, I was on the balcony. I looked through the windows. I could see chairs, a table, and a television. There was a door into a back room too, but no painting.

'Jamie, can you open the door? Sometimes they don't **lock**,' called Nadine from the garden.

She was right: the lock didn't work.

climb to go up or down using your hands and feet

balcony a place at the front of a building upstairs where you can stand and look out or sit in the sun

lock to close with a key; this makes a door stay closed

I opened the door easily and went into the flat. I was afraid. I didn't want Mr Williams to find me here. I looked quickly at the front room. Nothing interesting. I put my head into the back room. Black trousers on the bed. White shirt on a chair.

Then I saw something little and black on a table by the bed. It was a 'sat nav' – a **satellite navigator**. My dad has got a sat nav. It helps him to drive in Oman. It tells him, 'go right', or 'go left'. It tells him 'drive on this road'. It helps him to find new **places** – and to go back to old places. It's a very good thing for a new driver – or a driver in a new country – to have.

I **switched on** the sat nav. I looked at the pictures on it. It **showed** many different places in Oman. You can put in new places, too. After you go to a place, you can put it into your sat nav. Then the sat nav can help you to find that place again later.

I looked at the places on Mr Williams's sat nav. There were two coffee shops, the art exhibition hotel, a second hotel, 'Ali's house', 'George's house', 'my flat' and 'home'.

'My flat' and 'home'? Why did he put 'flat' and 'home'? I looked at 'my flat'. Yes, that was right. It was here. Then I looked at 'home'. It was in the **mountains**. Why? He didn't live there. There was a pen on the table. I quickly wrote the sat nav **information** about 'home' on my arm. Time to go before Mr Williams came home.

I climbed back over the balcony and down into the garden. Then I told the others what was on the sat nav.

'My mum's got a sat nav in her car,' said Nadine. 'I can bring it.'

She came back five minutes later with her mum's sat nav.

We put the information from my arm into it.

'Hmm. It's not very far. It's only thirty or forty minutes from Muscat by car,' said Taymour.

'There's not much there,' said Nadine. 'Only one road. No more buildings.'

'My parents want to go for a drive in the mountains this weekend. Perhaps we can drive to this place then. Let's ask them,' said Sarah.

'Can Taymour and I come too?' asked Nadine.

'And me,' said Ruth.

'It's a big car. We can all go,' said Sarah.

READING CHECK

Circle the correct words to complete the sentences.

a When he arrives home, Jamie speaks to **Sarah** / his mother / his father.

b The two men take a **photo / picture / woman** from the exhibition.

c The picture is very **big / expensive / beautiful**.

d The children go to Tom's **garden / office / car**.

e **Taymour / Jamie / Ruth** climbs up to the balcony and goes into Mr Williams's flat.

f In the flat, Jamie finds things to **eat / drink / wear** and a 'sat nav'.

g Mr Williams has a **friend / 'home' / child** in the mountains, Jamie learns.

h He writes the information about the building **on his hand / in a book / on his arm**.

i The children want to go to **Muscat / the mountains / the sea** and find the house.

WORD WORK

1 Use the pictures to help you complete the words from Chapter 5.

a p a i n t i n g

b _ _ i e _

c _ a _ _ o _ _

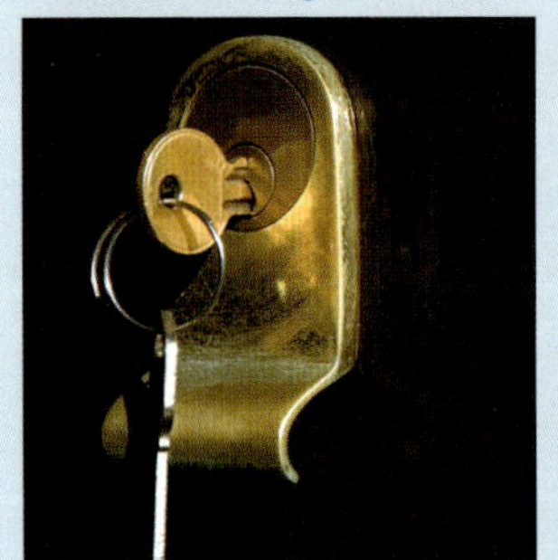

d _ o _ _

e _ a _ _ a _

f _ o u _ _ a i _

2 Match the first and second parts to make words.

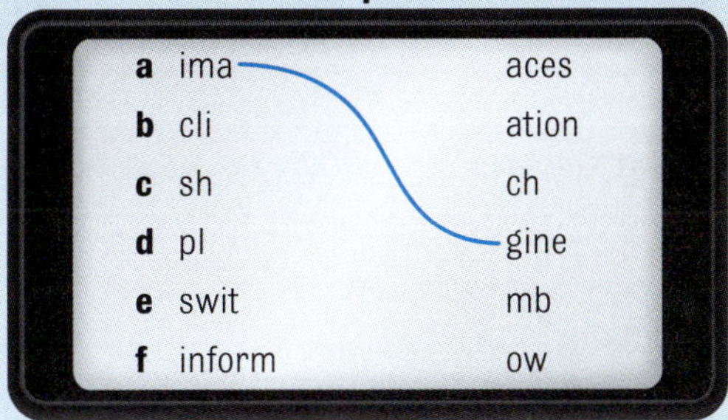

a	ima		aces
b	cli		ation
c	sh		ch
d	pl		gine
e	swit		mb
f	inform		ow

3 Complete the sentences with words from Activity 2.

a Jamie didn't …*imagine*… the conversation between the two men.

b I love visiting new …………………

c They looked in the newspaper for some ……………… about the men.

d They want to ……………… Mr Williams's flat to the police.

e It was easy for Jamie to ……………… up to the balcony.

f Can you ……………… on the TV? I want to see a film.

GUESS WHAT

What happens in the next chapter? Tick the boxes.

a The next day they go to … with Jamie's parents.

b They find the building with the help of … .

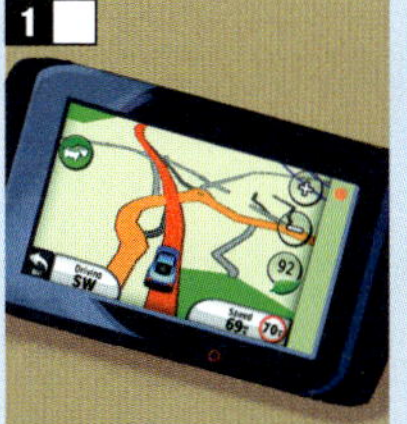

c They find … in the building.

d They drive away fast because of … .

Chapter 6 — Ruth's place

The next morning, Taymour, Nadine, and Ruth arrived at our house and quickly got into the car with Sarah, our parents, and me.

'We're going to the **museum** first. Then we're going to the mountains,' said my dad, with the sat nav in his hand.

'Can we go to *this* mountain?' I asked. I showed him the place on the sat nav. It said 'Ruth's place'.

'Is that Ruth's **favourite** place?' asked my dad.

'Yeah,' said Sarah.

'OK. We can look at it. And then we can stop for something to eat.'

The museum was interesting for my parents, but we kids wanted to go to 'Ruth's place' at once. I looked at my watch every five minutes. 'Are we going to be late? Is the painting going to be there?' I thought.

'Can we go to the mountains now, Dad?' asked Sarah.

'OK,' he said.

We all smiled. My dad put his hand on the sat nav. 'Here we go. "Ruth's place!"' We drove away from the museum. There were not many cars on the road.

'So, tell me about this place, Ruth. Why is it your favourite?' asked my dad.

'Erm, well, it's very quiet,' said Ruth.

My dad laughed. 'All Oman is quiet,' he said.

'And it's interesting, people say. Well, interesting for *us*,' said Ruth.

'Yes, very interesting,' said Nadine.

'Well, I want to see this very interesting place!' said my mum with a smile.

We drove for thirty minutes. There were no trees or

museum a building where people go to look at old things

favourite the one that someone likes best

buildings or people. Only mountains and the road. Then, in front of us we saw a little building.

'There it is!' Ruth cried.

'Is that it?' said my mum.

'What's interesting about this place?' asked my dad.

'Dad, can we stop the car?' I asked.

We all got out of the car. It was very hot.

'Mr Jackson, Mrs Jackson, look at the building,' said Nadine. 'It's very old. But it has **electricity**. There are lots of old buildings in the mountains in Oman, but they don't usually have electricity. Why does *this* building have it?'

The door didn't open. It had a lock on it. There was only one little window. My dad looked through it.

'I don't understand. It has air conditioning. Why is there air conditioning in this old building?' he asked.

'Dad, we know the answer. They need a cold building – for the *picture*.'

electricity
you need this to make TVs, computers and air conditioning work

33

'What are you talking about?' asked Mum.

'We've got something to tell you,' I said. We told them about when we overheard the two men on the balcony and about the painting in the art exhibition.

'At first we thought, "They want to kill someone!" – but in the end we understood the mystery. It was all about the painting,' said Sarah.

'And you didn't tell us before?' asked my mum. 'I'm not happy. You must always tell us about important things. And how did you find out about this place?'

'She's not going to be happy about that!' I thought.

'Mrs Jackson, Mr Jackson, can we go into the building?' asked Ruth quickly.

'Well, I have lots more questions, but yes. Let's go in,' said my dad.

He walked over to the door and **kicked** it. The lock **broke** and the door opened. We saw a large box in front of us. We opened it quickly. A woman's face looked back at us. It was the painting!

'Phone the police, Joe,' my mum said to my dad.

My dad put his hand in his trousers. But his phone wasn't there. He went back to the car. But the phone wasn't there.

'What happened? I had my phone earlier,' he said.

'Perhaps it's at home,' said my mum. 'Take my phone.'

'Dad, Mum, look! A car's coming!' cried Sarah suddenly.

Far away, there was a black car. It came quickly up the road to us.

'Oh, no! It's the thieves!' cried Taymour.

'We need to go. Quickly!' said my dad.

'Shall we take the picture with us?' I asked.

'No, let's leave it here – or the thieves are going to come after us in their car,' said my mum.

'Get into the car, everyone. Quick!' cried my dad.

When we drove away, my dad asked, 'Can you look for the nearest **police station** on the sat nav?'

'The nearest one is behind us, on this road,' said my mum, 'but we can't go there. The next one is about 30 kilometres away. We need to take the road to the airport.'

My dad drove very fast. But we could see the black car behind us. It didn't stop at the building. It came after us. My dad drove faster and faster. We left the mountains behind us. We drove past a hospital, and some houses. My dad drove slower now.

'Go left. Drive two kilometres,' said the sat nav.

'We're nearly there now, kids. The thieves aren't going to come after us down all these roads,' said my dad.

'And they're not going to drive to a police station with us,' said my mum.

We were very near the police station now. We found a place for our car, but then …

'Mr Jackson, look! It's them, in that car,' cried Taymour. The black car was not far away, and it came nearer.

police station
the building where the police work

'Quickly, everybody, into the police station,' said my mum.

We ran to the police station. There was a little building in front with only one police officer in it. He cried something in Arabic, but we didn't stop. We felt afraid. Soon we were at the door of the police station. The black car drove up to the little building. The car window came down and the driver said something to the police officer. Then the door of the car opened and a man got out. He was an Omani police officer, but not in a usual blue Omani police car!

He had a phone in his hand. My dad walked over to him. The police officer spoke to him in Arabic. My dad didn't understand. I couldn't understand. But the police officer spoke angrily to my dad. Taymour and Nadine smiled. Then Taymour ran over and helped my dad.

'You left your phone at the museum, he says. The people in the museum gave it to him, and he drove after you. He wanted to give back your phone. But you drive very fast, he says. He's not happy about that. You must drive slowly when you have children in the car, he says.'

'Taymour, can you tell him about the painting? I drove fast because I was afraid. We were in danger, I felt, and I wanted to get away from the thieves. I made a mistake about his car. It had a police officer in it, but I didn't know that. Tell him that.'

Fifteen minutes later, the police knew everything. Now they smiled. They took my dad back with them to the mountains. A young police officer drove me, Sarah, Mum, and our friends home. We waited for dad there. My mum phoned Taymour and Nadine's parents, and Ruth's parents too. 'Please come to our house,' my mum said. They were very angry when they first heard the story. 'Next time tell us everything,' they said. But, in the end, they told us, 'Good work, kids!'

Three hours later, my dad arrived home. We all asked him questions at the same time.

'OK. Wait a minute. Can I speak? The police have got the painting. They've got Mr Williams and his friend, too. They're very happy to find the picture. We must go to the police station tomorrow morning to tell them the story from the **beginning**.'

'From the beginning?' I said.

That was only a week ago. At that time I thought 'It's boring here!' but in the end it was the most exciting week of my life. I can't wait for next week!

READING CHECK

**1 Put these sentences about Chapter 6 in the correct order.
Number them 1–10.**

a ☐ Mr Jackson can't find his phone.

b ☐ The driver of the black car gives Mr Jackson's phone to him.

c ☐ After thirty minutes, they see a little building.

d ☐ Jamie tells his parents about the men and the painting.

e ☐ The children drive to a museum with Jamie's parents.

f ☐ They drive away fast after they see a black car.

g ☐ The sat nav helps Mr Jackson to drive to the mountains.

h ☐ The police find the painting and Mr Williams and his friend, too.

i ☐ They go into the building and find the painting.

j ☐ They stop their car and run into a police station.

WORD WORK

Correct the mistakes in the sentences.

a Jamie liked the exhibition of old daggers in the **minutes**. _museum_

b Nadine's **famous** animal is the dolphin.

c There's no **detective** in our house at the moment so we can't watch TV.

d Jamie's dad **kills** the door of the building and it opens.

e The next morning, they go to the police **office** and tell their story.

f The thief **spoke** the window to get into the house.

g I liked the **beginner** of the film, but I didn't like the end.

WHAT NEXT?

Read about two more *Mystery in Muscat* stories. What do you think happens? Which would you like to read next? Why?

It's winter in Oman and the five friends swim in the sea at the weekends. One day, they find a dead turtle with a dagger next to it. Who killed the turtle? Why did they do it? Can the friends find out before the killer finds more turtles?

The five friends overhear two women at the swimming pool. They are talking about an old car exhibition at a museum in Muscat. The next day thieves get into the museum and take the Sultan's silver car. Did the security guards see anything? Do the women know where the car is? Can the five friends find it?

Project A *Paintings of women*

1 Read about the painting and answer the questions.

This painting is of Mary Emily, Countess of Salisbury. The British artist, Sir Joshua Reynolds, painted it between 1780 and 1781. In the painting the countess is standing in the park near her country house. There are some tall trees behind her.

She's wearing a beautiful long brown and white dress. She has white hair. Rich people put white powder in their hair at this time. She's pulling on long yellow gloves. She's looking out at us, but she isn't smiling. She has her little dog next to her.

a Who's the painting of? .the Countess of Salisbury..

b Who painted the picture? ....

c When did he paint it? ....

d Where's the woman standing? ....

e What's behind her? ....

f What's she doing? ....

g What's next to her? ....

2 **Look at this painting of a woman.**
Answer the questions.

Painting of: English writer Vita
Sackville-West
Painter: William Strang (Scottish)
Painted: 1918

a Where is the woman sitting?

....

....

b What's behind her?

....

....

c What's she wearing?

....

....

d What's in her hand?

....

....

e Who's she looking at?

....

....

3 **Use the notes and your answers to write about the painting.**

Project B — *Travel guide*

1 Match the words with the pictures. Use a dictionary to help you. Circle them.

beach (h) / b   camels d / j   canyon b / f   desert e / i   fort f / c

mosque c / g   mountains h / a   oasis d / i   palm tree h / e   sand dunes g / a

❖ Top Things to See in Oman ❖

Wadi Ghul

Nizwa

Wadi Shab

Old Muscat

Mirbat

Sharqiya Sands

2 Read about Oman and complete the *Quick Facts* guide.

Oman Travel Guide

Overview
Information
Top Things to Do
Sightseeing
Getting There
Transport
Weather
Visa Information

Visit **the Sultanate of Oman** in the **Middle East**, in the southeast of the **Arabian Peninsula** for your holiday. You're never going to forget it!

The best time to visit is from October to early March. Summers are hot and humid with temperatures of up to 54°C.

Oman has a coast of almost 1,700 km on the **Indian Ocean** and the **Arabian Gulf**. See the beaches at **Sur** and the dunes at **Mirbat**, and swim with the turtles and dolphins in the beautiful blue sea.

Do you like mountain holidays? Oman has something for you. Visit mountain villages and beautiful canyons. See some of Oman's forts. (They're over 2,000 years old!) Climb to the fort at **Nizwa**, the country's capital in the 6th and 7th centuries, and look down on the city's beautiful mosque.

Do you prefer to travel in the desert? Then go by camel to **Sharqiya Sands**, or visit the **Wadi Shab** oasis and sit under the palms.

And at the beginning and end of your holiday, enjoy **Muscat**, Oman's beautiful capital city. You must visit the old fort and the **Sultan's Palace** on any visit to Oman!

Oman Quick Facts

Full name: ....
Location: ....
Capital city: ....
Weather: ....
Best time to visit: ....

Places to visit:

Place	What to see
Muscat	....
Mirbat	....
Nizwa	....
Sharqiya Sands	....
Sur	....
Wadi Shab	....

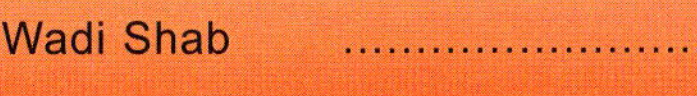

3 Use the *Quick Facts* to complete the web guide to Scotland.

Scotland Quick Facts

Name: Scotland
Location: Northern British Isles, with England to the south **Capital city:** Edinburgh
Weather: never very hot, can rain a lot in summer, snow in winter
Best time to visit: summer

Places to visit:

Place	What to see
Edinburgh	Edinburgh Castle, the Royal Mile (the most famous street)
The Highlands	Ben Nevis, highest mountain in Britain (1,344m), winter skiing in the Cairngorm mountains
Island of Skye (west coast)	Dunvegan Castle, Cuillin mountains, Portree town

Scotland Travel Guide

Visit .... in
.... for
your holiday. You're never going to forget it!

The best time to visit is in the ....

There are more than 100 Scottish islands. One
of the most beautiful is .... ,
off the ....
Visit .... Castle, the .... mountains, and
.... town there.

Do you like mountains? Scotland is the place for you! Climb ....
.... – the .... mountain in Britain. In winter, you can
go .... in the .... mountains.

And at the beginning and end of your visit, enjoy the capital ....
of Scotland, ... Be sure to visit Edinburgh
.... and see the Royal ....
– the .... street in Edinburgh when you're there.

4 Find out about another country and write a web travel guide about it.

Australia   CHINA   England
Lebanon

GRAMMAR CHECK

There was and ***there were***: **affirmative, negative, and questions**

We use there was and there were to talk about things and people that we could see in a place. We use there was with a singular or uncountable noun, and there were with a plural noun.

There was air conditioning in their house in Muscat.

There were lots of men in thobes and little white hats in Oman.

Negative forms are there wasn't and there weren't.

There wasn't air conditioning in their house back home.

There weren't lots of men in thobes in England.

Question forms are Was there …? and Were there …?

Was there a swimming pool across the road?

Were there gardens in front of the flats?

1 **Complete the sentences with *there was*, *there wasn't*, *there were*, or *there weren't*.**

a …There weren't… any friends at the airport to meet them.

b ……………………… a driver in a car in front of the airport.

c ……………………… any flats on the right of Tom's flat.

d ……………………… a hose in Tom's garden.

e ……………………… a swimming pool in Tom's garden.

f ……………………… two old garden chairs near the door to Tom's flat.

g ……………………… little turtles to see and dolphins to swim with in the winter.

2 **Complete the questions with *was there* or *were there*. Then write full sentences.**

a ……Was there…… English bread or Arab bread on the breakfast table?

…There was Arab bread on the breakfast table…………

b ……………………… three or four children in the swimming pool?

………………………………………………………………………

c ……………………… a lot or not much to do in Oman in the summer?

………………………………………………………………………

d ……………………… two men or two women in the first floor flat?

………………………………………………………………………

e ……………………… somebody or nobody in the flats next to Tom's flat?

………………………………………………………………………

GRAMMAR CHECK

Past Simple Yes/No questions and short answers

We use was/were or the auxiliary verbs did and could + infinitive without *to* in Yes/No questions in the Past Simple.

Did Jamie have any friends in Oman?   *Was Sarah happy to be in Muscat?*

Could Taymour and Nadine swim?

In the short answer we re-use the auxiliary verb or was/were.

No, he didn't (did not).   *No, she wasn't (was not).*   *Yes, they could.*

  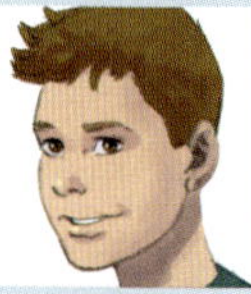  

3   Write answers for the questions using the short answers in the box.

> Yes, they could.   Yes, they were.   No, she wasn't.   No, she couldn't.   Yes, she did.
> No, they didn't.   Yes, they did.   Yes, he could.   No, they weren't.

a Were Taymour and Nadine from Oman?   ...No, they weren't...

b Could they speak Arabic, English, and French?   ....

c Were Taymour and Nadine twins?   ....

d Did they have dark hair and dark eyes?   ....

e Was Ruth from New Zealand?   ....

f Did Ruth have red hair?   ....

g Did Ruth's mum and dad work at the airport?   ....

h Could Ruth say a lot in Arabic?   ....

i Could Jamie go to Taymour's house?   ....

4   Now write short answers to these questions.

a Could Jamie and Taymour play on the computer all afternoon? ....

b Did Nadine help to water Tom's garden?   ....

c Was Tom Irish?   ....

d Was he in Scotland for the summer?   ....

e Did Taymour like watering Tom's garden?   ....

GRAMMAR CHECK

Information questions and question words

We use **question words** in information questions.

We answer these questions by giving some information.

Who is arriving from England on Friday?   The British Minister for Culture and the Arts.

Why is she coming to Oman?   Because she wants to see a big art exhibition there.

When does the exhibition open?   On Sunday.

5 Complete the information questions with the question words in the box.

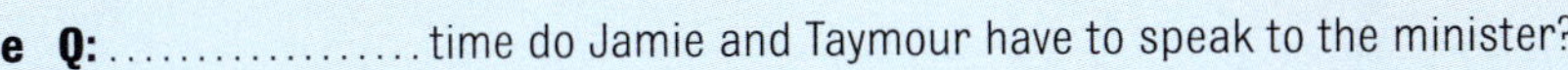

How	How much	How long	~~What~~
When	Where	Which	Who	Why

a Q: ..... *What* ..... is the exhibition of?

A: British and Omani pictures.

b Q: .... is the minister arriving on Friday?

A: Because there's going to be a VIP party on Saturday.

c Q: .... is going to be at the party?

A: The Sultan of Oman, the minister, and a lot of VIPs.

d Q: .... is the party going to be?

A: At one of the big hotels in Muscat.

e Q: .... time do Jamie and Taymour have to speak to the minister?

A: Two minutes.

f Q: .... is the minister staying in Oman?

A: Two nights.

g Q: .... is she going to leave Oman?

A: On Sunday morning.

h Q: .... country is she visiting after Oman?

A: China.

i Q: .... does the minister talk to Jamie and Taymour?

A: Nicely.

GRAMMAR CHECK

Adverbs of manner

We use adverbs of manner to talk about **how** we do things.

After some time the car stopped suddenly.   *'They're nice children,' said my mum noisily.*

We make adverbs from adjectives by add –ly.

sudden – suddenly

For adjectives ending in –y, we change y to i and add –ly.

noisy – noisily

Some adverbs are irregular.

Ruth spoke very fast. (adjective = fast)

Taymour and Nadine knew Oman well. (adjective = good)

6 **Use the adjectives in brackets to complete these sentences with adverbs of manner.**

a 'My mum never asks Nadine to do things,' said
   Taymour … *angrily* … (angry).

b 'I need to sit down,' I said .... (tired).

c Taymour and Jamie listened .... (quiet)
   to the men on the balcony.

d They didn't understand the conversation very
   .... (good) at first.

e 'I need a drink,' said Martin .... (thirsty).

f The kids couldn't speak .... (open) in
   front of Mr Williams.

g Taymour and Jamie looked .... (careful)
   at everyone in the hotel.

h 'It's a painting!' cried Ruth .... (excited).

i Jamie opened the door to Mr Williams's flat .... (easy).

j He looked at the information on the 'sat nav' .... (interested).

k 'A car's coming!' cried Sarah .... (sudden).

l Mr Jackson drove away from the building .... (fast).

m 'You didn't do .... (bad), kids,' said all their parents in the end.

GRAMMAR CHECK

Going to Future: affirmative and negative

We make the *going to* future with the verb be + going to + infinitive. We use the *going to* future for plans and intentions, and for predictions we make when we feel sure of something.

'We*'re going to live* in Muscat,' he told his family.

'We*'re not going to stay* in London,' said Mr Jackson.

'It*'s going to be* boring in Oman,' said Jamie.

'I*'m not going to have* any friends to play football with,' he told his mother.

7 **Complete these sentences with the verbs in the box in the *going to* future form.**

(not) arrive	(not) be	(not) believe	buy	drive	have
kill	look	see	(not) stay	~~(not) tell~~	water

a 'I *'m not going to tell you* again,' said Taymour's mum. 'You must water Tom's garden today.'

b 'Hey, Jamie! I . . . . you with this hose!' laughed Taymour.

c 'Nobody . . . . her again – here, or in England,' said George.

d 'I . . . . a long, expensive holiday,' said Mr Williams.

e 'I . . . . a big house by the sea,' answered George.

f 'Those men . . . . somebody,' whispered Taymour.

g 'The police . . . . our story,' said Jamie. 'They never believe kids.'

h 'We . . . . for the information in the *Oman Times*,' said Nadine.

i 'It . . . . easy to save her,' said Taymour.

j 'OK, kids. We . . . . long at the museum,' said Mr Jackson.

k 'And after that we . . . . into the mountains,' he told the children.

l 'Oh no! We . . . . at the building in time,' thought Jamie.

GRAMMAR CHECK

Past Simple: negative

To make the Past Simple negative we use **didn't** (**did not**) + **infinitive without *to*** for most verbs.

*The black car **didn't stop**.*

The Past Simple negative of be is **wasn't** (**was not**)/**weren't** (**were not**).

*The museum **wasn't** interesting for us kids.*   *There **weren't** many cars on the road.*

8 **Mark these sentences about the story T (True) or F (False). Make each false sentence true by writing the negative form of the verb.**

a Jamie and Sarah ~~swam~~ *didn't swim* with dolphins. [F]

b It was .... very hot in Muscat in the summer. [T]

c Taymour and Jamie overheard .... two thieves. ☐

d The girls learnt .... more about the mystery woman in the *Oman Times*. ☐

e The Minister for Culture and the Arts was .... a woman. ☐

f Mrs Summers was .... in terrible danger. ☐

g The kids met .... Mr Williams at Taymour and Nadine's house. ☐

h Taymour and Jamie spoke .... to Mrs Summers at the airport. ☐

i The kids were .... wrong about the hit-men. ☐

j The thieves took .... a painting of a man. ☐

k The building in the mountains had .... the painting in it. ☐

l Mr Jackson left .... his phone at home. ☐

m The thieves were .... in the black car. ☐

n The police found .... Mr Williams and his friend. ☐

GRAMMAR CHECK

Past Simple: irregular verbs

Irregular verbs have different Past Simple forms in the affirmative. You must learn them.

put – Jamie put *the information into the 'sat nav'.*

speak – The police officer spoke *to Dad in Arabic.*

make – We made *a mistake about the black car.*

9 Circle the Past Simple forms of these verbs.

a	be	**(was/were)**	been	**i**	go	gid	went
b	begin	began	begun	**j**	have	had	hove
c	break	brook	broke	**k**	leave	left	lave
d	drive	drove	driv	**l**	run	run	ran
e	feel	fole	felt	**m**	see	sed	saw
f	meet	met	meat	**n**	take	took	tade
g	get	got	gat	**o**	tell	telt	told
h	give	gove	gave	**p**	think	thought	thank

10 Complete Jamie's diary with the Past Simple forms of the verbs in brackets.

Saturday 29th

Today was an exciting day. Sarah and I a) ....got up.... (get up) early and Ruth, Taymour, and Nadine b) .... (meet) us at our house after breakfast. We all c) .... (feel) very excited. We d) .... (begin) the day at the museum with Mum and Dad. Dad e) .... (leave) his phone there by mistake! After that, Dad f) .... (take) us to the building in the mountains. It g) .... (be) old, but it h) .... (have) electricity and air conditioning in it. We i) .... (tell) Mum and Dad about the thieves. Then Dad j) .... (break) the lock on the door and we k) .... (go) in. We l) .... (find) the painting in a box there. Then Sarah m) .... (see) a black car on the road. 'It's the thieves,' we n) .... (think). So we o) .... (run) to our car and p) .... (drive) to a police station. The police q) .... (be) very happy when we r) .... (give) them the information about the painting and Mr Williams.